Sunshine Moonshine Baby

As far back as Sarah could remember there had been the sewing ladies. She hadn't seen them for a long time because she thought sewing was stupid.

But one evening she had to visit them, and they started telling her about life in far-away islands. The way they talked you'd think a different sun and moon shone there. The sun by day and the moon by night shone down on the islands that nestled like birds in the sea.

Sarah's eyes opened wider and wider . . . and soon even her dislike of sewing couldn't keep her away.

Sunshine Island Moonshine Baby

CLARE CHERRINGTON

Illustrated by Jennifer Northway

This edition published 1994 by
Diamond Books
77–85 Fulham Palace Road
Hammersmith, London W6 8JB

First published in Great Britain 1984 by
HarperCollins*Publishers*
First published in Fontana Lions 1985

ISBN 0 261 66485 9

Printed and bound in Great Britain

This book is dedicated to
Anna, Enid, Ethel, Gloria and Lynne
whose West Indian childhoods were
the inspiration for these stories

1

The Beginning

As far back as Sarah could remember, and further back than that, even, there were the sewing ladies. Suddenly one evening they would be in her grandmother's room downstairs, sitting in the big chairs, talking, sewing and laughing. And then they were gone again, and her grandmother's room seemed so empty. At first Sarah thought they just came and went when they felt like it. But when she grew older, she realized they came every Wednesday.

First there was Mrs Lily, who was thin and bright eyed as a bird, and so old she walked bent over. Mrs Wendell was plump and smiling, in a flowery dress,

and she always called Sarah "darling". Miss Hayes wasn't as old as the others, but she couldn't walk, so she sat down all the time in a wheelchair that Sarah called her magic chair because it seemed to move of its own accord. And then there was Sarah's grandmother, who was very strict, but could make you laugh more than anyone else in the world.

They made rag dolls in beautiful dresses or trouser suits, with innocent eyes and glass beads in their hair that jangled and clicked in your hands. Or they made animals—friendly big dogs with pink bows and yellow eyes that glowed like huge moons you could melt into. And koala bears whose eyes you couldn't find at all because the fur was so deep. And once Mrs Wendell made a huge lion, almost as big as Sarah's baby brother.

Sarah loved looking at the dolls and animals. But she got bored with the children's clothes they made, and the baby jackets they knitted, which all looked exactly the same. Besides, all the ladies ever said to her was how she'd grown and how pretty she looked. She would run off to play with her friend next door, goodbye, goodbye, goodbye!

But then she was ill. She had to go into hospital to have her tonsils out, and when she came home she wasn't allowed to go back to school. It was autumn, and everywhere full of fallen, broken leaves, but her mother wouldn't let her go outside and play. Time slowed down, stopped, and then began to go backwards.

She got very bored with playing on her own and helping her mother. One day she ended up crying at the foot of the stairs, where her grandmother found her.

"Stop that bawling," she said to Sarah. "You come along and sew with us tonight. That will give you something to do."

"I can't sew," Sarah protested.

"I was sewing when I was your age. Mrs Wendell was making dolls when she was your age. What is this word 'can't'?" Her grandmother looked straight at Sarah.

"I can't sew," she repeated, staring at her feet.

"You ever tried?"

"No."

"Don't you *ever* say you can't do something until you've tried! Tonight you sew with us. Come along straight after supper, mind!" And the old lady walked off, fierce and upright.

Sarah made a face. She'd rather be ill all over again than stuck in her grandmother's room with all those silly old women.

But it was no good. She was trying to disappear out of the kitchen after supper when her mother stopped her.

"Sarah! Didn't your grandmother invite you to her sewing group?"

"But Mummy, I can't sew."

"That's why you're going. She's going to teach you. Goodness, did the doctor take out your brains instead of your tonsils?"

"Sewing is stupid!"

"It's you who's stupid. Sewing is very useful."

"It's stupid," said Sarah. "Anyway, boys don't sew."

"But you're not a boy," her mother said. "Now— are you going to sew or going to bed?"

Reluctantly Sarah crept, slow as a snail, towards her grandmother's room. She could feel her mother watching her. Maybe someone would ring the door-bell just at that very instant and her mother would have to go and answer it. But nobody rang, and now she was holding the door handle. She twisted it, slowly, slowly, and then became very shy all of a sudden as eight sharp eyes looked at her all at once.

"Good girl! Come in, Sarah!" said her grandmother.

"So you're going to learn to sew, girl!" said Mrs Lily, patting the cushion next to her on the sofa. "Come and sit here."

"Go on then," said her grandmother.

Sarah felt trapped. She said "Hello" and crept over to the edge of the sofa and sat as far away from Mrs Lily as she politely could.

"You're the keenest sewer I've ever seen in my life," said Miss Hayes, smiling.

"She'll be fine once she's started," said Mrs Lily. The old woman turned to Sarah. "I'm going to teach you to thread a needle," she said, just like a teacher. Sarah watched as she took a piece of thread and a needle. Then she put the end of the thread through the tiny eye on the end of the needle, and pulled it through. "Now you try," she told Sarah.

Sarah tried, but although the thread started off in the right direction, when it got near the needle it swerved and missed the hole. She tried again, and the same thing happened. She wished God would

make all the needles in the world suddenly disappear.

"Oh, look at her face," broke out Mrs Wendell, who started laughing. And when she laughed she shook, which set all the flowers on her dress dancing. "Oh my Lord! Isn't she just like my daughter when she was small!" But then she noticed Sarah looking upset. "Don't you mind, darling," she said. "I was just taken a long way back, watching you."

"Did you really make dolls when you were little?" asked Sarah suddenly.

"Who told you that? Oh, I see," said Mrs Wendell, smiling at Sarah's grandmother. "Yes, I was selling dolls' dresses when I was your age."

"Didn't you go to school?" Sarah was shocked.

"Oh Lord, school! Yes, I went to school—when my mother didn't need me at home."

"None of this is helping Sarah thread her needle," Mrs Lily pointed out severely.

"My mother says school is more important than anything," Sarah said quickly.

Mrs Lily nodded her head. "Now she is quite right there. Nothing, but nothing, is more important than school, eh, Mrs Wendell?"

"That's right," said Mrs Wendell.

"Then why did your Mummy stop you going to school?" asked Sarah triumphantly.

"Things were different in Guyana, girl."

"Where is Guyana? Is it next door to Jamaica?" That was where Sarah's family had come from.

"Oh no, darling!" Mrs Wendell replied. "There is practically all the West Indies in the way."

"Mrs Wendell," broke in Mrs Lily. "Sarah has joined us to learn how to sew. Isn't that right?"

But Sarah just turned to Mrs Lily and asked, "Do

12

you know how many islands there are in the West Indies?"

"Of course I do, child!" Mrs Lily replied indignantly. "Let me see. There is Cuba, Jamaica, Puerto Rico, Haiti and Dominica, Guadeloupe, Basse Terre, Monserrat, Antigua —"

"The Virgin Islands," added her grandmother, "and the Dominican Republic, Martinique, St Lucia, St Vincent, Barbados —"

"Grenada, the Windward Islands and the Leeward Islands," put in Miss Hayes.

"And Trinidad and Tobago," finished Mrs Lily. "And there are many smaller ones. And then the Mainland."

Sarah felt that her head was an ocean, in which there were hundreds of islands swimming. But where was Guyana? Nobody had said Guyana? So she

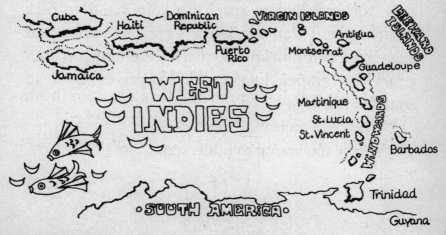

asked, and found it was in the continent of South America.

"And South America," said Mrs Wendell, "is big enough to tuck all the West Indies into a corner of it and lose them altogether!"

And Sarah wondered if it was as big as Africa, which someone at school had said was the biggest continent in the world.

But now they began talking about life in the islands. The way they talked, you would think there was a different sun shining over there, in a different sky that was always blue. And the moon was as bright as a thousand streetlamps. And the sun by day and the moon by night shone down on the islands that nestled like birds in the sea.

Sarah's eyes opened wider and wider as they talked about the different fruit that grew there, and how you just had to reach up your hand to pick whatever you wanted. There were star-apples and salsapples and pineapples, there were mangoes and pears and grapes, bananas and sugar cane. It all sounded lovely.

"Why did you leave?" she asked.

"You're too young to understand," said Mrs Lily.

Sarah was about to protest, when Mrs Wendell caught her eye.

"You know what we used to sing, Sarah, when we were little?"

Sarah shook her head.

Mrs Wendell began to sing, and the song went like this:

"This long time girl I never see you
This long time girl I never see you
This long time girl I never see you
Come let me hold your hand.

This long time girl I never touch you
This long time girl I never touch you
This long time girl I never touch you
Come let we reel and turn."

"I never thought I'd hear that again," said Mrs Lily. "It takes me right back to the beach, and the waves whispering, and Moonshine Baby. I used to love that."

"Sarah!" came her mother's voice from the corridor. "Time to go to bed."

"What is Moonshine Baby?" asked Sarah.

"Ah, we used to play such games," Mrs Lily went on, not hearing her.

"When you're a child, the whole of life seems like a game," said Miss Hayes.

"But what is Moonshine Baby?" Sarah asked again.

"Moonshine Baby —" Mrs Lily began.

But just then Sarah's mother came into the room. "Come on Sarah—bedtime!" she said.

"Can't I stay a bit longer?" Sarah begged.

"No. It's already past your bedtime. Say goodnight to the ladies, now."

"But I want to know what a Moonshine Baby is," Sarah protested.

"You come back next week and I'll tell you," said Mrs Lily. "And we'll get on with that sewing."

At the mention of sewing, Sarah quickly got off the sofa. They all said goodnight, and she went out with her mother. She suddenly felt awfully tired.

"That wasn't so bad, was it?" her mother said as they went upstairs. "And you're invited back next week. Aren't you lucky!"

Sarah wasn't so sure. But before she could make up her mind, she fell asleep and dreamed of islands and suns and moons, all swimming in a big blue sea. All night she dreamed. But just as someone in her dream was about to tell her what a Moonshine Baby was—she woke up! That was when she knew that she would have to go back to the sewing ladies to find out.

2

Moonshine Baby

By next Wednesday, however, Sarah wasn't so sure about visiting the sewing ladies. It would be so boring. And then her mother made it impossible anyway. They were all in the middle of having supper when her mother turned round to her father and said, "Did you know that the old ladies are teaching Sarah how to sew?"

Sarah was furious. "No, they're not, and I'm never going there again," she burst out.

Her father made a face at her mother and then began to talk about business, which was all he knew anything about. And Sarah decided to play in her room after supper.

So when she came out of the kitchen she padded softly, softly, softly, along the corridor towards the staircase. She was surprised to see her grandmother's door open, and then she heard Mrs Lily's voice, "Is that little grandchild of yours coming to join us this evening?"

Sarah tiptoed softly, softly, softly up the first few stairs, and heard her grandmother reply, "A foolish child. She's too stupid to sew and she's not interested in stories about Moonshine Babies and such."

Sarah stopped. She wasn't stupid, and she did want to hear about Moonshine Babies. But she was far too dignified to run down and tell them so.

"It's a pity," Miss Hayes said. "But kids are stupid. They don't even know what they enjoy until you tell them."

"Kids aren't stupid," Sarah shouted down. She was angry. "Grown-ups are stupid."

"Why?" shouted up Miss Hayes.

Sarah came downstairs to tell them. But when she got inside the door and felt them all looking at her, her courage fell to her feet, through the carpet and into the floorboards. She hung on to the door handle and felt silly.

"Why, hello there, Sarah!" said her grandmother. "Are you coming to join us?"

"Come and sit down," said Mrs Lily.

"Why are grown-ups stupid?" asked Miss Hayes.

"I don't know," said Sarah. And then she plucked up her courage and went and sat down right beside Mrs Lily and asked, "Will you tell me about the Moonshine Baby now, please?"

All the women laughed, and the flowers on Mrs Wendell's dress, which were yellow this week, were set dancing.

"I don't know about that," said Mrs Lily. "Wasn't there something about learning to sew?"

"Oh please!" begged Sarah.

"Well," said Mrs Lily, "I'll do a deal with you, Sarah, girl. You thread a needle, and I'll tell you a story."

Sarah thought about it. Threading a needle wasn't really sewing. Anyone could thread needles. "All right," she said.

And again the awful thread went to the right of the needle, and to the left, then to the right again, then it scrunched itself up just as it was about to go into the hole, then it went to the left again,

but at last, when she was about to give up, there it went, straight through the hole and the needle was threaded. "Look!" she cried out, holding it up triumphantly, "Look, look!"

Mrs Lily smiled. "Good girl," she said. "And now I've got to tell you how I used to play Moonshine Baby, eh?"

"Oh no," Sarah protested. "Tell me the story about Moonshine Baby."

"But child, that is a story."

"No, no, no," Sarah went on. "You have to tell a proper story, beginning, 'Once upon a time there was a little girl . . .' ".

"Ah—I see," said Mrs Lily. "Sure you don't want to tell the story yourself?"

"I don't know the story, so how can I tell it? And I did thread the needle," said Sarah.

"All right," said Mrs Lily, smiling. So she began: "Once upon a time there was a little girl, a little girl, a little girl called Estelle, which means star. And she lived in Kingston, which is the capital of Jamaica."

"Is that the same Jamaica you come from?" Sarah asked her grandmother.

"The very same. Now you be quiet and listen. She lived with her aunt and uncle."

"Why?"

"Because her mother had too many children to look after and her aunt and uncle didn't have any at all.

"Now Estelle was always asking questions, just like another little girl I know. She wanted to know why the sky is blue and why the sun shines. She wanted to know why birds sing and why trees grow up and not down, and why fish live in the sea. Everything that happened she would ask why, and if nothing was happening, she would ask about that, too. Questions seemed to fly out of her mouth like birds and perch everywhere.

"Her uncle and aunt were always answering questions, and so were the servants, who worked in the house, which was very big. The only person who never answered Estelle's questions was the dog, Mr Go. But he always came swimming with her in the sea which was just over the road. Her uncle would pick up an old car tyre and off they would go, with Mr Go running ahead. Then her uncle sat her in the tyre and spun her round. Round and round and round she went, bobbing up and down in the waves, until it seemed that the sun was dancing round her in the sky and throwing gold and silver coins on the water. And suddenly her uncle would shout at Mr Go, and he would swim up to Estelle, take the tyre in his mouth and swim back to shore.

"For Estelle was quite small and couldn't swim yet. All she ever did was ask questions. 'Why do you eat food?' 'Why can't I live for ever?' Some of the

answers she got were very strange, but she always got answers—until a certain day.

"That day was Sunday. Estelle was very excited. She was going to ride the Avenue tramcar. A tram is a sort of bus which runs on rails, and on Sunday afternoons the Avenue tramcar went all round Kingston for a penny, just for children.

"And there it was, and children were bursting out of it like sardines jumping out of a tin! They were laughing and shouting and singing, and Estelle only just squeezed on before it left. Off they rumbled among the cars, bicycles and people, up hill and down hill, along the edge of the sea and past the Myrtle Bank Hotel, as big as a mountain. They saw all of Kingston, and then when they were nearly back Estelle heard two girls talking about something called a Moonshine Baby. She was just going to ask them —"

"Oh please, what *is* a Moonshine Baby?" asked Sarah.

Everyone laughed.

"I said you were just like Estelle," said Mrs Lily, smiling.

And Sarah blushed.

"But just before Estelle could ask them," Mrs Lily went on, "the tram stopped, and the little girls ran off. So Estelle asked her aunt, but she didn't know, nor did her uncle or any of the servants. Even the vegetable seller who came to the back door didn't know. Nobody knew. Estelle couldn't understand it."

"She did find out, didn't she?" asked Sarah.

"Wait and see," said Mrs Lily. "Estelle didn't think she'd ever find out. Especially because, next thing, she had to go and visit her family in the country. She was excited to see her mother and father and brothers and sisters, and at first it was so nice, she forgot about Moonshine Babies. But then she got bored. There was nothing in the country except mud and cows and trees and plants, and every time you went out you got your clothes dirty. She had to help in the house, and help with the animals too—all the sorts of things the servants did in Kingston!

"It was no use expecting them to know about Moonshine Babies. And although once or twice she looked hopefully up at the big bright moon at night, half expecting to see a baby nestling there, she didn't really believe she would. No, the only babies in the countryside were real babies, and they kept popping up all over the place. A friend of her mother's had one while she was there, and she went and watched them plant a tree for it. All the fruit on the tree would belong to that child. Her brothers and sisters had trees of their own too, but she didn't, because she was born in Kingston.

"At last the three weeks' holiday was over, and she went back to Kingston. But by now she had begun to enjoy playing in the countryside, and had quite forgotten about Moonshine Babies. It was Christmastime, and the John Canoe dancers were going round the houses, acting, singing and asking for money. Then it was Christmas Day itself! Her aunt, her uncle and Estelle all went down to Victoria market to buy toys for her. This one, this one and that one! You could see them all lined up on the ground. And the children ran around with little whistles with feathers on them, whistling like birds, so that everyone's ears rang for hours afterwards.

"After they left Victoria market, they took the boat for Port Royal. Now Port Royal —"

"But I want to hear about Moonshine Baby,"

cried Sarah. "Estelle's forgotten all about it."

"Hush—let me tell the story. Sarah, if you ask one more question I will stop."

"I'm sorry," said Sarah.

"Now Port Royal," Mrs Lily went on, "was an old pirate city. Pirates always have hideouts on land, and the West Indies used to be full of pirates. You see, there were all these big ships passing by, with gold and jewels going from South America to Europe. The most famous pirate was Captain Henry Morgan—and long, long ago, Port Royal was his hideout.

"It was a wild, wicked city then, full of pirates fighting and drinking. But then an earthquake shook it, and most of it fell down, and then a fire burned down most of the rest. After that there wasn't much left of Port Royal. Only grass, where the castle used to be, and way, way down in the sea there were cannons. Estelle used to stare at them down through the clear water, until she came all over dreamy and had to jump up and run about to shake off the long-ago feeling.

"They stayed at Port Royal until the big red sun went down, and the big yellow moon rose to hang like a lamp in the sky, lighting up the sea with a silver light. Everything was still and quiet. There was just the rocking of the sea and the crackling of the fire where her aunt was baking fish for a picnic supper.

"Then suddenly the night was full of people and children. The children swept Estelle up with them, and they all ran off to another part of the beach. She knew some of the children from Kingston, so she wasn't afraid. Then they asked her to lie down in the sand, because she was the smallest child there. As she lay there she felt them putting things all round her.

Then they told her to get up, slowly and carefully.

"So she did, and when she looked down she saw lots of pretty pieces of broken china that shone and glittered in the moonlight. They were laid out in the shape of a child on the sand—or it might have been a —"

"Moonshine Baby!" Sarah cried out.

"Exactly." Mrs Lily nodded. "They had made a Moonshine Baby by putting the shiny bits of china all round her as she lay on the sand. And that's how she learned what a Moonshine Baby was. She was so pleased —"

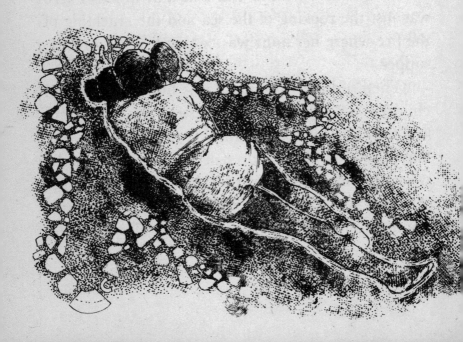

"Sarah!" her mother called from the corridor.

"So pleased she wouldn't leave it. Estelle cried when they tried to take up the bits of china, and the other children left her there and went off to play Sally Water. But Estelle just sat by her beautiful Moonshine Baby. And after supper, when her aunt and uncle went to look for her, there she was, fast asleep. They picked her up —"

Sarah's mother peered round the door. "Bedtime," she said.

"And they carried her to the boat and home to bed. And that is the end of the story," said Mrs Lily, firmly.

Sarah's mother came into the room. But Sarah wouldn't go. She sat stubbornly on the edge of the sofa. "What is Sally Water?" she asked.

"Sarah!" all the ladies chorused at once. Sarah suddenly felt very small.

"There is no end to this child's curiosity," said her grandmother. "You will have to find the answer in your dreams, Sarah."

"You must let the ladies get on with their sewing," said her mother, reaching out a hand. At once Sarah jumped off the sofa.

"Goodnight," she said, sleepily. "Thank you."

"Will we be seeing you next week, then?" asked Mrs Wendell.

"I expect so," her mother said quickly. "She's so keen on the sewing."

"Goodnight, goodnight," said Sarah, pulling her mother out of the room. Halfway upstairs she declared, "I'm never going to sew, ever, ever again. All I'm going to do is make Moonshine Babies."

But life is full of surprises.

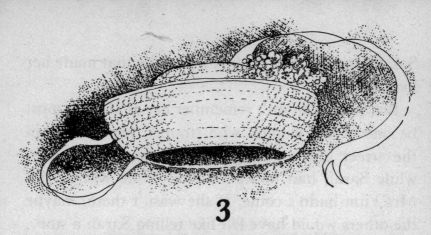

3

The Most Beautiful Girl
in Jamaica

As you may remember, Sarah had no intention of
ever going back to the sewing ladies. But it is one
thing to make a decision—and another to keep to it!
When it came round to next Wednesday evening,
Sarah thought maybe she just ought to go and say
hello to the sewing ladies so they wouldn't be dis-
appointed.

She almost didn't notice the stranger sitting in a
corner in a smart dark blue suit and hat. "This is
Mrs Finn," said her grandmother.

At once Mrs Finn started talking. "I remember
you when all you could do was bawl!" she told

Sarah, and her eyes flashed in a smile that made her look beautiful.

But Sarah couldn't remember her at all. She must be one of the women who stopped her mother in the street and had long conversations with her, while Sarah had to wait politely. She wished this Mrs Finn hadn't come. If she wasn't there, maybe the others would have felt like telling Sarah a story. But now they would just talk among themselves. She stared at the floor.

"Well, girl!" said Mrs Finn. "Is this all the welcome I get?"

"Hello," said Sarah.

Mrs Finn looked round at the others, with her eyes wide open in surprise. "I shall go right on back home! This girl doesn't want to hear any stories."

"Stories?" asked Sarah.

"That's what I said."

"D'you know any stories?" asked Sarah.

Her grandmother smiled. "Mrs Finn's got more stories than a centipede has legs."

"Oh please tell me a story," Sarah begged. She ran to sit down on the sofa.

"That's all very well, girl," said Mrs Finn, "but

what sort of story d'you want? One about fish or birds, soldiers or thieves, spacemen or shopkeepers, witches or princesses?"

Sarah shook her head. "I want a story about a little girl."

Mrs Finn frowned. "I don't think I know any stories about little girls. Little boys, yes, but little girls, no."

"Oh yes you do," said Miss Hayes. "A story about a little girl who lived in Kingston, Jamaica."

Mrs Finn frowned deep in thought. Suddenly she smiled and her face lit up. "All right, child," she said to Sarah. "I'll tell you a story about a little girl called...called Annie-Mae, who lived in Kingston Town. This little girl wanted just one thing—to be the most beautiful girl in all Jamaica.

"Now Kingston was very different in those days. Now it is full of modern buildings, cars, hotels, and that kind of thing, but when Annie-Mae was young, they still had carts on the streets and lived in old houses.

"Annie-Mae was very pretty and very thin. She lived with her brothers and mother and uncle and grandmother in a big house with a veranda at the back. Now, it was the mango season, which is in June, and it was blazing hot, too hot to sleep. Every evening they sat out on the veranda, fanning themselves till late at night.

"At school it was hot, too. Annie-Mae and her friend, Gloria, cut themselves fans out of cardboard. 'Ooo it's hot, Annie-Mae, it's hot in here,' Gloria said, fanning herself.

"And Annie-Mae answered, 'Yes Gloria, it's hot in here, whoo!' And at the end of the day they ran out and bought themselves snowballs, which weren't made of snow at all, but bits of ice rolled up in a ball with syrup poured over them. And as they walked home, they talked about what they wanted to be when they grew up. Gloria wanted to be a nurse, but Annie-Mae was going to be the most beautiful girl in all Jamaica.

"It didn't seem very likely that all Jamaica would ever hear of Annie-Mae. The only person in their family who was at all well-known was her Uncle Joshua, and he was only famous for one day a year. That was when he collected his firm's money off the boat from England. He'd drive back from the docks in a cart with a carload of police in front and behind him. All the time people would shout, 'Uncle Joshua, Uncle Joshua, throw that box of money over here!'

" 'While I'm driving, man?' Uncle Joshua shouted.

" 'Never mind that, man. Throw it down! Quickly!'

" 'You want them to shoot me in the back?' Uncle Joshua shouted, and drove on. He never threw the box down. And the rest of the year people didn't pay him much attention, so you couldn't really call him famous.

"But he was always nice to Annie-Mae. When he came home in the evening he had fruit or sweets for her—pear or coconut, soda-cake, brilla-cake or coco-bread with butter inside. It was often past Annie-Mae's bedtime, and her mother shouted, 'Annie-Mae, Annie-Mae, go to bed now.'

"But Uncle Joshua answered, 'I want her to sew on a button for me; please let her stay.' And so she did, and often didn't get to bed on time. But it was summer and it didn't matter.

" 'Gloria, I tell you, I will be the most beautiful girl in all Jamaica,' said Annie-Mae, fanning herself. 'So don't you bother laughing at me.'

"But Gloria did laugh. 'I tell you what you are. You are the skinniest girl in all Jamaica. If you aren't careful you'll break!'

" 'You watch your words,' said Annie-Mae. 'I have a memory like . . . like a giraffe.'

"Gloria ran off giggling. But Annie-Mae remembered.

"Now every Sunday, all the children went to

38

church with their parents. And all the girls were dressed up very pretty, with ribbons around their dresses and ribbons on their hats. All these ribbons were very tempting.... And next Sunday Annie-Mae just happened to find herself sitting behind Gloria and her cousin, looking at their ribbons flowing down behind them. So in a quiet moment she gently tied the ribbons of their hats together.

"Nobody noticed. And then it was time for the hymn. Everybody stood up and Gloria and her cousin's hats shot off into the air and everyone looked round. But all they saw was Annie-Mae in her pretty white dress singing 'Gloooooory!' like a little angel. People whispered, children laughed, and the parson shouted, 'Quiet, quiet!' and Annie-Mae just went on singing as if butter wouldn't melt in her mouth.

"'Annie-Mae,' Gloria said to her after the service, 'you are the naughtiest girl in the whole of Jamaica.'

"'And when I grow up I'll be the prettiest,' said Annie-Mae, sticking out her tongue.

"But she was growing up all the time. That autumn her mother had a great fight with her schoolteacher, and then sent her to a different school. Next summer she had a real fan, and looked down on silly little girls who ate snowballs and cut themselves fans out of cardboard. And when she went to church it wasn't to tie hat ribbons together. Oh no! Annie-Mae went to church to show off her beautiful clothes."

"That's silly!" said Sarah.

"That's what every girl does when she grows older," replied Mrs Finn. "You'll do it—wait and see!"

"No I won't. I never, never will. I hate dolls and pretty clothes. I like doing things, not dressing up!"

"Goodness me! Take it easy. There's a reason for girls to look pretty," Mrs Finn went on. "If you don't bother about it, what sort of husband will you get when you grow up?"

"I'm never going to marry," said Sarah. "I'm

going to be a cowboy."

"I see," said Mrs Finn. "Well, there weren't any cows in Kingston, so Annie-Mae couldn't be a cowboy even if she had wanted to be. Besides, her mother always said if she didn't marry when she grew up, she'd have to sew for her living. And Annie-Mae didn't like sewing any more than you do. So she wanted to marry. And if you want a good husband, you have to dress nicely."

"Why?" asked Sarah.

"Because men only like pretty women."

"Then men are stupid," said Sarah.

"That may well be true," said Mrs Finn, "but they can also be very nice. And besides—you are forgetting she wanted to be the most beautiful girl in all Jamaica.

"She already was almost the prettiest girl in her church. There was only one who excelled her. This girl's name was Harriet, and she came from a rich family who could afford to buy her all the dresses she wanted. Annie-Mae was always begging her mother to buy her new dresses and the answer was almost always no, they couldn't afford it.

"It was the mango season again, and it was

blazing hot! At night they sat up fanning themselves on the veranda until late, late! Soon it would be the church festival and Annie-Mae begged her mother to buy her a new dress.

" 'I tell you I can't afford it!' said her mother. 'Now quit bothering me, child.'

"Now Annie-Mae's mother was the most stubborn woman in the whole of Kingston, and when she said no, she meant it. But Annie-Mae took after her, and when she said no, she meant it too. 'Then I'm not going to the church festival,' said Annie-Mae, and stomped off.

"Her mother did not want to carry her to church. And besides, Annie-Mae was her only daughter. And on the day before the festival, she said, 'Come here, child. We're going in to Kingston to buy you a new hat.'

"They went to Mr Clark, one of the best dress-makers in Kingston. He was one of those men who walk and talk like a woman, although they are men.

" 'Oh Mr Clark, Mr Clark,' said Annie-Mae's mother, 'tomorrow's the big festival at church and I haven't got a new hat for Annie-Mae. And she says she'll shame me and not go to church and I haven't got a penny on me at the moment. And I wondered —'.

" 'Don't you worry,' interrupted Mr Clark. 'You just come into my shop, you and Annie-Mae, and I'll find her a hat.'

"And he made her such a beautiful hat. It was pink, with little pink flowers on one side and a long single ribbon flowing down the other. This was called a 'come-follow-me' ribbon, because it was what the girls wore when they went dating. With this hat on, Annie-Mae looked like someone in a movie. And she knew it!

"And so did Mr Clark and her mother.

" 'Now you take that hat off and guard it with your life,' said her mother suddenly. Then they left, with Annie-Mae clutching the hat so tightly that Mr

Clark laughed and asked if she thought it would fly away.

"Annie-Mae just looked at him scornfully, but that night she dreamed the hat grew feathers and ran off, flapping its wings like a chicken. Round and round the kitchen she chased it, but just as she was about to catch it, it jumped out of the window and began to fly away. Quickly she ran outside and tried to catch it by the long ribbon. But when she got it, the ribbon just came away in her hands and the hat flew higher. Then the moon came out, and way up there she could see it laughing at her with Harriet's face, and as she shook her fist at it, she saw it was now wearing her hat.

"She woke up crying. But, when she looked round, there, safe beside her bed, was the beautiful

hat. Daylight was coming through the window and she could hear her mother in the kitchen. It was only a dream!

"She jumped up, put on her white dress like any other Sunday, and then put on the hat.

" 'Oh Annie-Mae you look pretty today,' said one of her brothers as she came into the kitchen.

" 'Pretty? The girl is beautiful in that hat!' said Uncle Joshua, and turned to her mother, 'How much did you pay for it?'

" 'Hush,' said her mother, and then raised her voice. 'All right, children, let's go.'

"Annie-Mae walked through the streets and felt as if she was in a film. Everywhere she looked, people were looking back at her. 'Is that Annie-Mae?' said someone. 'She's grown up overnight,' someone else replied. When she got to the church she felt like a princess and walked up the steps with her head held high.

"But then she heard Harriet's voice behind her. For a moment she felt afraid. But then she just wheeled round with her long ribbon, and stood there.

" 'Oh Annie-Mae,' said Harriet, 'what a beautiful hat. Where did you get it?'

"Annie-Mae just shrugged her shoulders and looked away.

"And then her Uncle Joshua said, 'Beautiful? Of course it's beautiful. It's worn by the most beautiful girl in all Jamaica.' "

Mrs Finn was quiet for a moment, lost in her dreams.

"Bedtime, Sarah," called her mother from the corridor.

"Annie-Mae was walking on air," Mrs Finn went on. "No one could compare her to Harriet any longer. But her mother spent weeks working extra to pay for the hat."

Sarah's mother came into the room. She was just about to pick Sarah up when she noticed Mrs Finn. "Hello," she said. "I didn't know you were here."

"I've almost finished the story," said Mrs Finn. "There is just one last thing, Sarah. When Annie-Mae grew older and left school, Mr Clark took her on to model clothes for him, so that her picture did get all over Jamaica! And she never did have to sew for a living, for she made the best marriage in the world. And that is all, girl, and you must go to bed."

"That story sounds familiar," said Sarah's mother.

"It's my story," Sarah protested. "Especially for me."

"Oh I see," said her mother. "Are you coming to bed now?"

Sarah wished Mrs Finn would tell her stories for

ever, but she was looking so distant now that Sarah didn't want to disturb her. Instead she jumped off the sofa and said goodnight to the ladies and followed her mother upstairs.

But halfway up she said, "I'm never going to look beautiful or get married. I'm going to be a cowboy and never wear a dress again."

"We'll see about that," said her mother.

4
The Island
and the Donkey

"I can't do it, I'll never be able to do it, and it's no use trying," said Sarah angrily, and she put down her sewing. This time she had joined the sewing ladies hoping Mrs Finn would be there again, but she wasn't. And now Mrs Lily expected her to sew two bits of material together and she couldn't. She wished the sewing ladies would vanish back into the furniture.

"Sit back a moment, then try again," said Mrs Lily.

Then Miss Hayes glided up to the edge of the sofa in her silent wheelchair. "If you can do it," she said, "I'll tell you a story!"

That did it! Sarah picked up the awful sewing and began stitching again. This time the two pieces of material magically became one. "Look, look!" she cried, holding it up.

"Good girl," said Miss Hayes. "I knew you could. Now, will you keep quiet while I tell my story?"

Sarah sat quiet as a mouse.

"There was a little girl," Miss Hayes began, "born on an island as round as a biscuit. This island was so small, that when you climbed to the top of the mountain in the middle, you would see the sea all around. The sea was a most beautiful blue; sometimes emerald, sometimes turquoise, and sometimes as deep and mysterious as a dream. And this little girl lived so close to it that she could hear the waves as they came in to land. That was the song of the sea, and it mingled with the song of the wind in the palm trees so that often it seemed to her that everything was singing.

"That was her music. Now everyone knows music is good when you feel sad, and this little girl was often sad. You see, her feet didn't have any toes, so she couldn't walk, or run and play with the other children. So she loved that music all the more.

"This little girl was called ... what was she called now? She was called Mary, and the island was one of the Windward Islands. Her family lived in a wooden house, all on the same level, not squashed up in one of these upstairs downstairs houses you have here. Outside, there were flowerbeds with roses, oleanders and hibiscus.

"There were many other peoples on the island. There were the Windward people whose skins were very light, Mulattos, who were a sort of suntan colour, and Indians from India, besides Black people. However, it didn't matter what colour you were: kids got flogged and grown-ups worked all the time, and that was that!

"When Mary was a baby she crawled around to play with her brother and sister. But when they started running everywhere, she got left behind. One day she was sitting alone by the palm trees. She watched the clouds changing shape over the sea, and the little white sailing boats skimming over the sea, and it seemed to her that everything except her was moving. All she could do was cry big tears and listen to the beautiful soft, slow, sad music of the sea and the wind in the palms.

"That night, when her mother tucked her up in bed, Mary asked, 'Why didn't God give me proper feet? I want to run!'

"Her mother looked at her for a moment as if she was going to cry. But then she smiled and sat down beside Mary. 'God has his reasons,' she said. 'One day you'll understand. But for now, make the best of it.'

" 'Everyone else can run,' said Mary, starting to cry.

" 'Don't you ever let God see you crying about the way He made you, child!' said her mother. 'If it's good enough for Him, it's good enough for you. You be content with what you have. Do you hear me crying because God didn't make me rich?'

"Mary sniffed. That was true.

" 'Now what were you and the others singing?' asked her mother. 'Was it this I heard?' And her mother began to sing, and soon Mary joined in....

" 'Sally, Sally Water
    Water in the saucer' "

"It's Sally Water!" Sarah cried out. "I forgot all about Sally Water. It's a song!"

"Hush," said her grandmother, and Miss Hayes went on singing.

" 'Rise, Sally, rise
    And dry your weeping eyes
    Rise, Sally, rise
    And take your choice.

Sally turn to the right,
Sally turn to the left,
Sally turn to the very one
You love the best.'

"Mary cheered up with the music, and now she began to sing her mother a song she'd just learned, which went like this:

" 'I've just arrived from Alambay, Alambay,
      Alambay
   To buy a concertina
   What is your intention, intention, intention
   My intention is to marry
   When you see a pretty one, a pretty one,
      a pretty one
   Put your finger out and call them
   That's the way my money goes,
      my money goes, my money goes
   To buy a concertina!'

"After that they both laughed and Mary's mother kissed her and said goodnight. Mary listened to the crickets sing in the darkness out there, with the sea and the palm tree song in the distance. Two fireflies flitted into the room and played, little moving sparks of light. Then they were gone. But by then she was asleep.

"A few days later her mother called her. 'Mary, Mary, look what Grandad's bought you.'

"Mary bumped along on her bottom, which was how she got about. There in the yard was her grandfather, and beside him was—a donkey!

" 'This is for you,' he told Mary. 'He's called Prince. He'll be your legs.'

"Mary stared and stared and stared. She didn't understand. Her brother and sister didn't have donkeys. Was she getting one just because of her bad feet? How nice the world was, all of a sudden.

" 'Well, child,' said her mother, 'haven't you anything to say?'"

" 'Give her time,' said her grandfather. He turned to Mary. 'Like to sit up on him?'

"Mary nodded.

"Her grandfather lifted her up and ever so gently put her on the donkey's back. It was broad and warm. She sat with one leg each side and it didn't matter any more that she couldn't stand. She could see so far, now. She was so tall.... Suddenly she got frightened and her grandfather took her down.

"But soon she was on the donkey all the time. She learnt how to get him to go the way she wanted. Now, in the morning, she just called 'Prince' and he came running to the back yard, and her mother put her on his back.

"They went all over the island. Mary learned how small, small, small it was. Everywhere was green. Mango trees green, palm trees green, coconut trees green, sugar cane green. 'Green, green, I love you green,' she thought when she was riding. That came out of a poem her grandfather read to her. Sometimes, as she was half-dreaming, riding along the secret, hidden paths, a bird flew out from the trees and startled her. A turkey, perhaps, or a red or yellow bird. Sometimes she stopped to watch a hummingbird, so small that if you caught it you could hold it in your hands. They hovered, with wings flapping so fast they hummed, and they sucked honey from flowers with their long beaks.

"She loved the secret paths among the trees. But best of all she loved going to visit her grandmother with her brother and sister. This was difficult enough for people with good feet, but if you were on a donkey, God help you! Because the path was so steep and rocky, there was nowhere for the donkey to get a foothold. Prince slipped and slid all over the place, and Mary just held on and prayed that she wouldn't fall off. Her sister steered from in front and her brother pushed Prince from behind, and up they went and down they slid and up again, laughing and shouting, until suddenly they were at the top. And there was grandmother with sweets for them all.

"But when they got home, Mary's mother was angry.

" 'Don't you take Mary up on the rocks on that donkey!' she shouted at them, 'or I'll give you all a flogging!' "

"Did she ever fall off?" asked Sarah.

"Children!" exclaimed Miss Hayes. "D'you want her to fall off? And her with bad feet?"

"Not really," said Sarah. "But maybe she did? Just once?"

"Maybe the moon will wink at you tonight," said Miss Hayes in a way Sarah didn't know if she was serious or joking. "Can I go on?"

Sarah nodded.

"Well," said Miss Hayes, "as you can imagine, there came a time when Mary wanted to go and see her grandmother, but her brother and sister weren't around. Instead of sensibly waiting till they came back, she decided she'd go on her own. So she called to Prince, and her mother helped her on.

" 'Where are you going?' asked her mother.

" 'Oh, just over there!' Mary pointed at some trees.

"Her mother was suspicious. Mary always said exactly where she was going. 'You're not going to see grandmother —?' she began. But just then the dog started barking, and her mother went over to see what it was.

"Mary set off at once. In no time at all she was at the rocky path. How steep it was! It made her feel all shaky inside. Prince kept trying to turn round and go back, but she made him go on. Steeper and steeper it got, and they began to slip and slide. Mary began to wish she hadn't come. But she couldn't go back now. It was all she could do to hang on to Prince. Then she began to feel herself slipping. . . .

"Suddenly she flew off his back! Then she couldn't

remember any more.

"When Mary came round, her head hurt and her shoulder too. At first she was just glad she was alive, but then she began to get scared. Prince wasn't anywhere around. And there were all sorts of strange, scary noises. She wished she was at home. She tried to move along on her bottom, but she hurt too much. All she could do was wait until someone came to find her.

"She never knew the day could be so long. But suddenly it got dark, and that was worse. She began to think maybe no one would find her. Then she saw a huge animal above her waiting to pounce on her ... until she realized what she thought were eyes, were only stars. It was horrible in the dark.

"But suddenly there were human voices. 'Mary,

Mary, where are you, child?'

" 'Here, I'm over here,' she shouted back, so loud that she was frightened at the noise.

"There were her father, grandfather and Prince. Her father bent over and picked her up and hugged her. Mary was so happy she couldn't say anything at all. She just felt a warm glow inside. She was all right. There were no wild animals and she would soon see her mother. But in fact she fell asleep long before she got home.

"However, the next day —"

"Sarah!" came her mother's voice from the corridor. "Bedtime!"

"What happened?" asked Sarah quickly.

"The next day—oooh, didn't she get a flogging!" said Miss Hayes. "Mary's mother told her if she ever went there alone again they would take Prince away, and she wouldn't be able to get anywhere at all! But Mary had learned her lesson, and was just glad to be home safe. And that, Sarah, is that."

"You make that flogging sound very real," said Sarah's mother, who had just come into the room.

"I don't know how I did that," said Miss Hayes. "I was far too good ever to get flogged," and she smiled at Sarah.

Sarah wondered for a moment. But she had another question. "How did they know where to find her?" she asked.

"Aaaah," Miss Hayes replied. "That's the question."

"Did her mother know where she was?"

"Maybe," said Miss Hayes. "Or maybe the donkey remembered the way. You think about it."

"Come on, Sarah!" her mother held out a hand.

Sarah jumped off the sofa and said goodnight and thank you to the sewing ladies. She suddenly felt very tired. As they went upstairs, she murmured to her mother, "I think it was the donkey that went to find her."

"Went to find who?" asked her mother.

"Mary," said Sarah. "It was a story about a little girl called Mary who had bad feet and rode a donkey."

"I think I've heard that story before," said her mother, as they went into Sarah's room.

But Sarah was too tired to wonder how that could be.

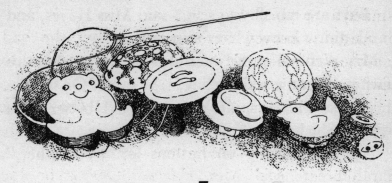

5

The End of the Beginning

"Every girl must be able to sew on buttons," said Mrs Lily. It was another Wednesday and you can guess where Sarah was. Now it seemed quite natural for her to be with the sewing ladies. "Just think," Mrs Lily went on, "you could sew a button on your brother's baby jacket."

Sarah put down the sewing at once. In fact, it wasn't really sewing. It was just a button and a piece of cloth all tangled up in thread. "He can sew on his own buttons when he gets bigger," she said.

"Boys don't sew," said Mrs Lily.

"Why not?" asked Sarah.

"Boys are too silly to sew," said Miss Hayes, and Sarah didn't know what to say to that.

Mrs Wendell came over and picked up Sarah's sewing. "Let me see, darling," she said. "Oh dear— this looks like a spider's web. We'd better start again." She began to cut the button loose.

"I'm not sewing on buttons for my brother," Sarah threatened.

"You don't have to, darling," said Mrs Wendell. "Just sew this one on for us."

"I'm too little," protested Sarah.

"You know what," said Miss Hayes, smiling. "You'll have to tell her a story, Mrs Wendell."

"Oh dear me, no," said Mrs Wendell, going back to her seat and picking up her sewing. Sarah suddenly noticed how fast Mrs Wendell sewed. The needle almost seemed to move of its own accord.

"Oh please, tell me a story," begged Sarah. "I'll try and sew the button on properly."

Mrs Wendell gave a shrug of her big plump shoulders. "Darling, I don't know any stories," she said. "I'm very sorry."

"Tell her the one about the little girl in Georgetown," said her grandmother.

"Oh no," said Mrs Wendell. "I couldn't."

"Oh please!" begged Sarah.

"You wouldn't be interested," said Mrs Wendell.

"Yes I would. Please tell me. What was she called?"

"Oh Lord!" Mrs Wendell rubbed a hand over her forehead. "How did this happen to me? I've never told a story in my life."

"Oh thank you," said Sarah. "I knew you would."

"You have a go at the button then," said Mrs Wendell, "and then I'll have a go at a story."

Sarah tried again and this time it worked! She ran to show the button and cloth to Mrs Wendell, who said, "Have I got to begin now?"

"Yes please," said Sarah, running back to the sofa.

"Well," said Mrs Wendell. "Let me see now. This little girl was called . . . called . . . Flora, and she lived in Georgetown. D'you know where that is, darling?"

Sarah shook her head.

"It's in Guyana. D'you remember where that is?"

"In South America!" replied Sarah.

"Good girl! So she lived in Georgetown. It's a big city with lots of people, and some of them so poor you could use their ribs for a xylophone. It's a hard life in Georgetown.

"Flora was small, and she smiled a lot. And she was different to other girls I know in that she loved sewing. She would have spent all her time sewing, if she didn't have to go to school and help her mother at home. Whenever she could, she crept into her father's workroom and sewed. For her father was a tailor, you see. And while he made suits and grown-up clothes, Flora made dolls' dresses out of scraps of material.

66

"The family was poor and it was just as well Flora liked sewing because there were no toys for her and her brothers to play with. But while her father was alive, they always had enough to eat. However, he died when she was still little. And then they were hungry. Soon they went to live with her uncle and his wife.

"Phew, but her Uncle Bob was an excitable man! 'You won't be poor for long with me around,' he said to Flora and her mother and brothers. 'I'm going to make a million dollars!'

" 'You said that last year,' his wife replied.

" 'That was nothing. This is the year,' said Uncle Bob. 'I'll have these children driven to school in a Cadillac. And a diamond necklace for Flora.'

"Flora's eyes grew wider as she listened.

" 'I'll believe it when I see it,' said her aunt.

" 'This time I can't lose,' said Uncle Bob. 'You heard of white Barbados goats? Babies go crazy over their milk. I'll buy some goats, and all over Georgetown babies'll be drinking Bob's Barbados Milk. You wait and see!'

" 'If they don't die straightaway,' mocked Aunt Mabel.

" 'If Moses had no faith, where would he have got?' replied Uncle Bob, going out.

"Flora didn't know who to believe. She wouldn't mind a diamond necklace. But she'd prefer a doll. Because she had all these dolls' dresses and no doll to put them on.

"She was sewing all the time now. But there was no one to give her scraps of material any longer so she cut bits off old clothes when they were drying. And she had no thread. She had to unwind little pieces off her mother's cotton reels. She would not stop sewing for anything! Once her mother caught her cutting a bit out of an old dress. 'Girl, you will leave me without anything to wear!' she screamed at Flora, and flogged her. But then she gave her the rest of the dress. 'Children must have a toy,' she said.

"So Uncle Bob sent off for the goats. And Flora's mother sold fruit to schoolchildren and took in laundry.

"Sometimes Flora stayed home from school to help her. They went to Starbrook Market, where big boats unloaded goods from all over the West Indies. The boats hooted, the men shouted as they unloaded goods, the stallholders shouted at their customers

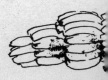

and the customers shouted back at the stallholders. It was pandemonium! Sarah loved it. You could see every sort of fruit and vegetable there—sugar cane and banana, grapes and mangoes, pears, pineapples, star-apples, salsapples, coconuts...and many more. Often Flora was given a little piece of fruit to taste.

"Back home they cut the fruit into little bits and arranged it on a tray so that Flora's mother could take and sell the fruit to the children.

"And how they all waited for the goats! At last they arrived. The back yard was suddenly full of them—noisy, smelly, dirty and naughty. Aunt Mabel wrinkled up her nose and milked them. The milk tasted warm and strange. At first it sold well, but then slower and slower, until soon they weren't selling any at all.

"It was supper time. They were all very quiet.

" 'We must eat these goats, Bob,' said Aunt Mabel.

" 'Beautiful white goats like that!' said Uncle Bob. 'Never! The people of Georgetown don't know what's good for them.'

" 'Go out and get a job,' said Aunt Mabel. And they began to row.

"That night Flora cried and cried. She had really half-believed she would get a diamond necklace, you see. She was tired of being poor and her mother working all the time. How silly it was being a child when you couldn't work for money. And then she had an idea.

"She made the most beautiful doll's dress she had ever made and took it to school. A girl in the class above her bought it. With the money Flora bought some thread of her own, and made another dress. She sold that, too, and began to save up the money.

"About that time they ate the goats, and her uncle left to go looking for diamonds up the Cayuni and Mazeruni rivers. 'You wait,' he said to them with his mouth full of goat's meat, 'I'll come back covered in diamonds!' But no one believed him any more.

"After he left, Flora's aunt went to work too, and Flora had to stay back from school and keep house for her brothers. She hardly had any time to sew, and thought it would be years before she saved up a dollar. She had to sweep, wash and help cook for everyone. But she wasn't sad, because she used to sing."

And at this Mrs Wendell got up and swept Sarah along to dance with her while she sang:

"Here comes the bluebird through the window
Here comes the bluebird through the door
Here comes the bluebird through the window

Take a little one and dance in the middle
Take a little one and dance in the middle
Take a little one and dance in the middle
Hey diddle-um-dee-day!"

"And that was what Flora sang as she washed and scrubbed, polished and brushed, chopped and stirred," said Mrs Wendell, going back to her chair, as Sarah ran to the sofa. "But one day, when she was putting the red wax on the floor, there was a shouting from outside!

" 'Diamonds! I found diamonds! We're rich!' It was Uncle Bob. He raced into the kitchen in a new suit and twirled Flora around. 'Where's everyone?' he asked.

" 'Working,' said Flora.

" 'Working—huh!' said Uncle Bob. 'Not with me around.'

"This time he really had got some money. That night he and Aunt Mabel had such a row! Uncle Bob wanted to buy a Cadillac, but in the end Aunt Mabel made him buy a small café instead. 'Business pays better than pleasure,' she said. So that was that. Flora's mother stopped taking in laundry, Flora was sent back to school—and nobody needed the 95 cents she had saved up!

"But Flora didn't mind. She went and bought

herself a most beautiful doll, of just the right size to model dolls' dresses. She was the happiest little girl in the world. It was Christmas Eve and they all sat together in the kitchen, watching the masquerade of dancers in the night. The drumming was so loud and fast you couldn't think at all. It seemed the whole city was dancing out there. There was a man with a horse's head, here an angel, there a devil leaping, then a man on stilts, a man with a cow's head on. . . . All these and more dancers came swirling up out of the night and disappeared back into the crowd

again. It was like a dream—and in fact, in the middle of it, Flora drifted off to sleep.

"Next morning when she woke up, she thought her Uncle Bob had only come back in a dream. But then why could she hear Aunt Mabel shouting 'Bob! Bob, come here!' "

"Sarah!" called Sarah's mother from the corridor.

"Her uncle was there," said Mrs Wendell. "And it was Christmas day too! And now, Sarah, you must go to bed, and my story is finished."

"What a lovely story," said Sarah, who had gone very quiet. Then she asked, "How did he find the diamonds?"

"He never told us," said Mrs Wendell. "I mean he never told Flora." And she took up her sewing again and looked as if she had never opened her mouth.

But Sarah looked straight at Mrs Wendell and asked, "What did Flora do when she grew up?"

"She did sewing, of course."

"And did she live in Georgetown all her life?"

"Off to bed with you!" said her grandmother. At the same time Sarah's mother came in. "Come on, Sarah!" she said.

But Sarah wouldn't leave off her questions. "Was Flora you when you were little?" she asked Mrs Wendell.

"She's cunning, this one," laughed Miss Hayes.

"What makes you think that?" asked Mrs Lily.

"Because of the sewing," said Sarah. "It is, isn't it? And because it was your uncle," she said to Mrs Wendell.

"She's got you there," said Miss Hayes.

"I suppose you have, girl!" said Mrs Wendell.

"I was right, I was right!" sang Sarah, jumping off the sofa. "Flora's Mrs Wendell."

"Does anything else come to mind?" asked her mother, looking at Sarah.

"What should that be, now?" asked her grandmother.

Sarah thought, and suddenly she realized what it was. "They were all you!" she said, looking round at the sewing ladies. Miss Hayes was grinning mischievously at her. "You were Mary, and your mother flogged you because you were naughty," she said.

"Maybe!" said Miss Hayes with her eyes flashing. "But it was fun on that donkey!"

Sarah turned to her mother. "And Mrs Finn was

Annie-Mae, the most beautiful girl in Jamaica."

"She still is beautiful, isn't she?" said her mother.

Sarah turned to Mrs Lily. "And you were Estelle," she said. "You played Moonshine Baby and asked questions all the time."

"Until I learned to look for the answers inside myself," replied Mrs Lily, "as you will learn to do."

"That'll be the day!" said her grandmother.

"Do you wish you were little again?" Sarah suddenly asked the ladies.

"This child is due for bed," said her grandmother.

"Come on Sarah," her mother said.

"But do you?" Sarah went on.

"Goodnight Sarah!" said Mrs Lily and the other ladies.

Suddenly they all looked very old and serious, sitting there sewing in the big chairs. Sarah went to join her mother. "Goodnight," she said, and they both went out.

"Goodnight, darling," came Mrs Wendell's voice as they started up the stairs.

Halfway up, Sarah said to her mother, "But I think they sometimes wish they were little again."

"Do you?" said her mother. "I wonder. It's not so bad being a child sometimes, eh?"

But Sarah didn't reply.

"There's something I do know, though," her mother went on. "The doctor says you can go back to school next week. Isn't that nice."

"I don't want to go back to school," said Sarah, suddenly feeling very tired and small. "I want to go to Port Royal and play Moonshine Baby. And to the

Windward Islands, and Kingston Town and —"

"Goodness me," said her mother, picking her up and carrying her into her room, "you have been getting ideas. If you do well at school, now, and get a good job, you'll be able to visit the West Indies."

"But I want to go now," said Sarah.

"Then," said her mother, "you'll have to visit it in your dreams."

But next morning Sarah couldn't remember her dreams, so she never knew if she had dreamed of the West Indies. That day she was allowed out to play, and met her best friend again. They told each other everything that had happened since Sarah had got ill. All weekend they played together, and then Sarah went back to school on Monday. Slowly she began to forget about the sewing ladies and their stories. They were different to the stories at school. And besides, sewing was stupid.

When next Wednesday came round, her friend asked Sarah over to play. So after supper she asked her mother if she could go. "Maybe I ought to go to the sewing ladies," she said.

"What d'you want to do most?" asked her mother.

"Go and play," said Sarah, staring at the ground.

"But they told me all those stories."

"Why not say hello to them, and then go and play," her mother suggested.

So Sarah did.

The ladies looked different tonight. They looked older and slower.

"Hello, darling," said Mrs Wendell.

"I came to say goodbye," said Sarah.

"I hear you're better," said Miss Hayes.

"Yes," said Sarah.

"I don't expect you want to sit talking to a bunch of old women," said Mrs Lily. "You'd better run off and play."

Sarah smiled. It was all right. "Yes," she said, going to the door. And then she turned round. "Thank you for all the stories." And she ran off to play with her friend, goodbye, goodbye, goodbye!

And that is the end of the story, because Sarah never went to listen to the sewing ladies tell their stories again.

And if you had asked her, she would have said she'd forgotten all about the little girls who lived in the sunshine islands. But some little girls from her school were found playing Moonshine Baby in the sand next summer.

And sometimes, when the girls skipped two or three at a time over a big rope with one end tied to a lamp-post, some of the words they sang had a familiar sound.

> This long time girl I never see you
> Come let me hold your hand. . . .

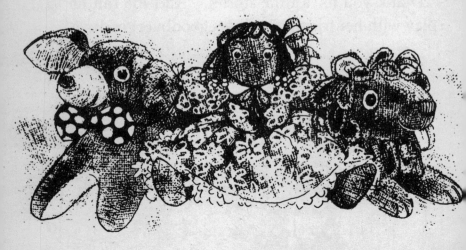